MW00808702

.

Saint Brigid and the Cows

Saint Brigid and the Cows

by

Eva K. Betz

Illustrated by

Russell Peterson

Neumann Press
Charlotte, North Carolina

Easy Reading Books of
SAINTS AND FRIENDLY BEASTS

Nihil Obstat:

    Frank J. Rodimer

        Censor Deputatus

Imprimatur:

    ✠ James J. Navagh

        Bishop of Paterson

June 24, 1964

Saint Brigid and the Cows

ISBN: 978-1-930873-95-7

Printed and bound in the United States of America.

Neumann Press
Charlotte, North Carolina
www.NeumannPress.com
2013

For
Margaret,
Sister,
and Fran

A flat rock on the hillside offered a comfortable seat, and Brigid sat down on it with a sigh. The warm surface felt pleasant against her bare feet as she tucked them under her. Then she smoothed her crimson skirt with its purple stripes and looked around her.

She had been hurrying about her work since sunrise and now she was ready for a rest. The cows she had driven up the hillside to graze were moving about the field but she knew that none of them would stray—they never did, when she was tending them, no matter how much they might desire at other times to get lost. Just as even the most skittish among them stood quietly when Brigid was milking.

She began to recite her lessons, and when that was done, she took a bundle of rushes she had gathered and plaited them into crosses. She sang little hymns as she plaited, songs of love and praise. A small calf walked over and nuzzled her as if pleased that she was honoring God.

Brigid was the daughter of a king, but as was often done in those days, she had been sent to live with a wise teacher and his wife. She had been with them ever since she was small. She was learning to speak clearly and well, to sing the songs of her country, Ireland, and to know about its history. There were other things to learn, too. Looking after a house, minding cows and sheep, making butter and cheese. A king's daughter needed to know how everything was done, even though she would have plenty of people to work for her in her father's castle.

Brigid was born in Ireland in the year 452. In those days Ireland was divided into many parts, each ruled by a chief or king. The king was rich and the people who lived in the castle with him and fought for him were well taken care of. But there were many, many others who were not so lucky. These homeless ones wandered from place to place looking for work. Most of the time they could not find any, so they had to beg their meals and sleep in the fields.

In the summer that was not so bad. There were wild berries and fruit to go with the crusts people gave them and the warm sky for a blanket at night. But in the winter Brigid used often to get

up at night and pray to the Baby born in a stable that He would give shelter to all the other homeless children, too.

Now, while she sat on her rock in the sun, a little breeze ran up the meadow. The flowers bent in a gay dance and the silvery undersides of the grasses turned up. On the breeze came the sound of jingling bells and the plop of horses' hoofs and the rumble of chariot wheels moving along the dusty road which passed the foot of the hill.

"A party going to the castle," Brigid said to herself. "Golden bells on the ladies' horses and the men and women all dressed so fine !"

She watched the gay party as it passed, saw the em-broi-dered gloves on the ladies' hands, their fine linen head-bands and the jeweled clasps of their cloaks. Some of them wore their hair in braids caught at the end with bands of gold. Others had their hair piled high on their heads and held with jeweled

combs. Tears came to Brigid's eyes as she thought of all the food that could have been bought for poor people with this finery.

When the party had ridden past, Brigid looked around again. She saw the red and yellow and purple flowers growing wild in the pasture land, and the blue sky overhead, and she began to sing once more. The song was not one she had learned from her teacher. His songs were all about wars and battles. This was her own kind of song, and the one she liked best. It was a song to Mary, the Mother of God, and it told how much Brigid loved her and the Baby Jesus. While she sang, the cows stopped grazing and quietly moved nearer to her.

When Brigid spoke, her voice was soft and low, as was proper for a king's daughter. But when she sang, her voice was high and strong, and as clear as the voice of a lark. She was a beautiful little girl always, but when she sang to Our Lady she seemed to become even more beautiful because of the love in her face.

"I must go back to the dairy now," she said to the cows when she had finished her song. "You be good creatures and don't stray off into the woods or the marshes. I wouldn't want you to get lost." The cows seemed to listen to her, and she knew that they would do as she said. They always did.

In the dairy, the milk the cows had given that morning stood in big earthen jars. There were twelve jars all the same size, and one very big one. The twelve jars Brigid called the Twelve Apostles. The big one she named for Our Lord, and that one held the milk she set aside for poor people who came begging.

So many of them came—more each week, it seemed. Brigid wished she had more to give them, but none went away without at least something. And to each she gave one of the little crosses she made from reeds and rushes. When she gave the cross, she took a moment or two to remind them of Christ the Lord. He, too, she would explain, was homeless and hungry. Homeless unless they took Him into their hearts, hungry for their love.

Brigid set to work. There was much to be done in the dairy. Sometimes it was shaping the great cheeses that would be stored in the cool cave in the hillside close by. At other times it was churning the cream into butter, as she was doing now. While she worked, she began to sing again.

"Christ be in my dairy," she sang. "Christ be in all the rooms of my house and in my heart!"

Up and down, up and down, went the handle of the churn. It didn't seem possible that slim arms could go so fast.

"Mary smile on my churning," she sang, "and be pleased with what I do!"

There was a scratching at the door and a little face peeped in. It was a child come begging, a child so hungry and tired that he looked more like a little old man. Brigid knew that he and his mother were sheltering in a rocky glen not far away.

"Come in, little one, come in," she whispered. Her teacher was not a generous man and he did not like Brigid's sharing his goods with the poor.

"Here. Drink a mug of this good, rich milk," she said, "and take this cheese home to your mother. And this bit of butter, too."

The little boy drank the milk, thanked Brigid, and ran off with the wonderful gifts.

More poor people came to the dairy during the day. And the next day more came. And the day after that, still more.

One evening when Brigid had finished her lessons, her teacher told her to wait a moment. The dancing flames of the fire did not give much light, but even so, she could see that he was angry.

"I met a friend on the road today, Brigid," he said, "and he laughed at me."

He paused as if he expected Brigid to say something. When she did not, he went on.

"This man said I was a fool. He said all the scoundrels in the countryside were being fed with my food."

"Scoundrels?" Brigid was shocked. "The poor whom God loves so much are scoundrels just because they are poor?"

"Of course they are scoundrels, or they would support themselves and not go begging from people who work hard! And if, as you say, God loves them so much, let Him feed them. I won't."

He stared fiercely at Brigid.

"I will go into the cave in the morning," he went on, "and

count the cheeses and the tubs of butter. You may be sure I know what the number should be."

"It is your cave," Brigid agreed, "and it is your cows that give the milk for the cheese and butter. But it is God who gives the grass to feed the cows, remember." And she walked quietly out of the room.

"The girl doesn't seem frightened," muttered the man to his patient wife. "Yet if what my friend told me is true, all our butter and cheese is gone. The cave must be empty."

The next morning, before Brigid took the cows to pasture, he came to the dairy.

"Now, then," he said, "come with me to the cave, and let me see all the fine butter and cheese you have made, and how nicely you have stored it!"

He set off to the cave carrying a rushlight in his hand, and Brigid followed him.

"Oh, lovely Mary," she prayed, "speak to your Son. Ask Him to bless the products of my dairy."

When he reached the center of the cave, the old teacher stood upright. He held the burning rush high so that its light showed him everything. He was amazed by what he saw.

Hanging from hooks in the stone were globes of cheese—many more than he had expected. And beside the running stream that cooled the cave were tubs of beautiful golden butter. There was so much butter that it seemed as if his herd of cows must be twice the size it really was.

He gasped, but said nothing. He just turned on his heel and went out of the cave, leaving Brigid to make her own way out into daylight.

"I don't understand it," he mumbled to himself. "My friend would not deceive me. He told me that pounds and pounds of but-

ter and scores of cheeses had been given away. Yet I saw for myself what a lot is stored there. I just don't understand what is going on!"

Meanwhile Brigid finished her work in the dairy. She took the cows to pasture, and there she settled down on her favorite stone.

She had many friends in the fields, little furred and feathered creatures which had discovered that Brigid loved them and that they were safe with her. They had their own ways of showing that they trusted her.

A mother fox came out of the woods bringing her three little cubs for Brigid to admire. A gray mole stole from his tunnel and let Brigid stroke his velvet back. A blackbird chose a branch very near her to sing his song. It was a beautiful day. Brigid spent it happily playing with the friendly animals, talking to God about them, singing to Our Lady.

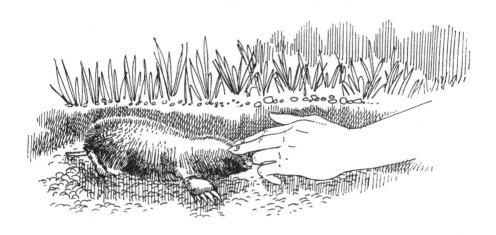

But behind her happiness, she felt a little lonely. No other people lived near her teacher's house, and Brigid would have liked so much to have other boys and girls to play with and talk to. And families often had babies! Brigid longed to cuddle a baby. The little animals were soft and sweet. But a real baby—that was what she would love to hold.

Once, before she had left her father's castle, she had been allowed to hold a baby. And sometimes now she saw beggar women going along the road with babies in their arms. She thought that no one was really poor who had a baby to love.

As Brigid was thinking about these things, a little wind

brushed the grass and a sweet smell filled the air. She looked up and saw a lady walking toward her. The lady was so lovely that Brigid wanted to cry. Folded in the lady's blue cloak she carried a baby surely the most beautiful baby that ever was seen!

Half of Brigid's mind told her that it was the Lady Mary and that the baby was Little Jesus. But it was almost too great a thing to think of or believe. She stood up and greeted the Lady, and then extended her arms.

"Could I—could I hold the Baby?" she asked very softly so as not to waken Him.

With a smile the Lady held the Baby out. And Brigid took Him. In her own two hands she cradled the Lamb of God!

The movement woke Him. He opened His eyes and smiled. Reaching up with one little hand, He took hold of a braid that lay across Brigid's shoulder. Then, safe and comfortable, He fell asleep again. The Lord God of Heaven was sleeping in Brigid's arms!

Brigid did not know if it was a moment or an hour that she held Him, because time seemed to stop. Then she gave Him back to His Mother. Mary wrapped Him in her blue robe again and went silently away across the fields.

The cows had not pulled so much as a blade of grass while the two Visitors were there. They had stood noiseless and very still. Now, they moved their heads and made soft mooing sounds as if they were talking about the Ones who had called on Brigid.

Brigid gazed at her hands. They looked just as they always had, but she felt that they must be changed. And she felt sure, too, that God had special work for those hands to do.

After this she noticed the world around her even more than she had done before, and she wondered about it. She wondered if God had laughed when He made the rabbits with their long ears, twitching noses, and funny little white tails. She wondered if He had planned every flower separately, and every tree. What a wonderful world He had made, if only people would keep it so!

The days came to an end which Brigid could spend on the hillside with the gentle cows she loved. Her time for learning lessons were over. She was nearly grown up. She must go home and take her place in her father's castle.

Brigid often wondered what it would be like. "I must try to please my father," she said to herself, "and do everything for him that a daughter should. But I do hope he won't want me to give my time to dancing and feasting. I want to spend my life serving God."

Her teacher had another idea about what might happen when she went back; back to a place where there was plenty of food and plenty of everything else all of which, he was sure, Brigid would want to give away. True, he himself did not seem to have lost anything through her generosity. But just the same he thought it only fair to warn her father.

When the day came at last for going home, Brigid put on her

cloak and said good-bye to the sheep, and the furry wild folk, and above all, the cows. Then she and her teacher set off for her home. When they had arrived and been made welcome, the teacher took her father aside.

"I must warn you, sire," he said, "that you must watch your daughter carefully."

"Watch her? Why?"

"Because she gives things away."

"Gives things away? What things?"

"Whatever she can get her hands on. She would give your whole castle to the poor if it could be managed."

The king burst out laughing.

"Oh, I don't think I need worry," he said. "She will have plenty to keep her busy now. Beautiful clothes, grand parties—and before long I will arrange a marriage for her."

"H-m-m," said the teacher doubtfully. "Well, I warned you."

The king's own house was set on a little rise of ground, and clustered about it were other houses and all sorts of buildings. There was the forge where iron workers made lance-tips and shields. There were the rooms where goldsmiths made beautiful ornaments for

men and women to wear. There was a weaving shed and a build-
ing where the dyers worked. All these buildings, together with the
king's house, were separated from the rest of the world by a wide
marsh through which a single road ran. The whole group of buildings was called the castle.

Life in this place was strange to Brigid. She had seen the visitors going to the castle when she spent days on the hills but she had been quite small when she went to live with her teacher. Meals there had been mostly oatmeal, milk, cakes of wheaten flour, with once in a while a bit of fish caught in the stream.

But in the castle there would sometimes be half an ox and several small pigs cooked for one meal. There was always butter for the bread, and many kinds of sweetmeats made with honey. While dinner went on, a minstrel would play on his harp and sing songs of love and of war. Or sometimes a juggler would perform, keeping flashing knives dancing in the air. How they glinted in the blaze of the candles that lit the hall!

The long evenings were given up to feasting and singing, end-

less talk, and the telling of stories. The ladies spent the whole of their days—or so it seemed to Brigid—in making themselves beautiful. They had all sorts of little boxes and bottles containing different things to put on their faces. There were colors and stains for reddening lips and cheeks and darkening eyebrows, and so on. And as the serving maids painted on new faces, the ladies studied the result in the nearest thing they had to mirrors—polished metal. Then their long hair had to be brushed and dressed and hung with hollow golden balls.

Brigid saw all this with astonishment. How could people waste so much time and trouble on anything so unimportant as their faces? And the money they spent on all this could have been used to house and feed hundreds in real need. Brigid herself had a beauty that none of these painted ladies could match. It must have annoyed them that she always looked so lovely, and never gave a thought to it!

As time went on, many of the young men who came to the court fell in love with Brigid. One after another asked her father if he might marry her. But Brigid refused them all.

"I do not want to marry," she told her father. "I am going to give my life to Christ."

Her father was determined that she should marry, but he was willing to wait a while.

"She will fall in love presently," he thought, "and then it will be a different story."

So he did not worry about it. But something else began to worry him. It seemed that things were disappearing in the strangest way. The special kind of meat he ordered cooked for a banquet was not there. The otter-skin robe for a guest's bed could not be found. And where was Brigid's new cloak? Suddenly he remembered what Brigid's teacher had said about her habit of giving things away.

He sent for her—she was in the cowbarn helping a herdsman with a sick animal—and spoke sternly.

"What do you know about all this disappearing and losing?" he asked.

"Why," said Brigid, "poor people are always coming and begging at the gate. Of course I give them things. They need them much more than we do."

Her father scolded her, but it did no good. Things continued to disappear, and at last the king lost his temper completely.

"It is high time you were married and had a home of your own," he said. "Then you will be more thrifty. It is right to be generous, of course but..."

"Father," Brigid interrupted, "I have told you I will never marry. Nor do I want to own anything anything at all. I want to give my life to Christ. He will provide all I need."

"Nonsense," said the king. "Of course you must marry."

Soon after this, he heard that a young prince who lived not far away was looking for a bride.

"Just the husband for Brigid," he thought. "A good man, strong and brave, and just the right age. I shall arrange this marriage for her whether she likes it or not."

It annoyed him that he had to send out to the fields for his daughter. When she came in, he told her what he planned. Then he called her maid and ordered the girl to dress Brigid in proper fashion for a visit to the prince.

"Oh, dear!" thought Brigid. She was quite sure she was not going to marry anyone, whatever her father arranged. But she couldn't refuse to go with him.

So after her maid had brushed her hair until it shone, Brigid was dressed in her finest gown. But her father directed that she was to wear no jewels. "Even when I am with her," he thought, "she will manage to give them away."

Brigid took her place beside her father in his chariot and away they drove to the home of Dunlaing, the prince whom her father hoped she would marry.

"And if he doesn't want you for a wife," he said, "I'll sell you to him for a slave. So you had better do your best to please him."

This was an important visit, so Brigid's father was dressed in his finest clothes and wore his most magnificent sword. The blade

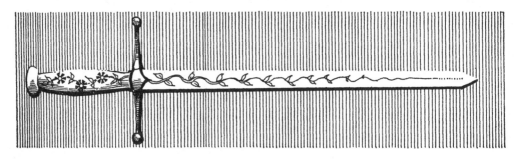

was brightly polished, and all down its length there was a golden vine set into the metal. On the hilt of the sword were jewels, arranged to look like flowers on the vine.

But it would not be polite to arrive for a visit wearing a sword—not even such a sword as that. So when Brigid's father went into Dunlaing's house to explain why he had come, he left it on the seat of the chariot beside Brigid. It sparkled in the sun and Brigid sat looking at it while she waited for her father.

Presently a beggar came along the road. His face was thin and white, for he was very ill and very hungry. "An alms, good lady," implored the man. "Give me a coin so that I can buy food and medicine."

Brigid's heart melted as she looked at him.

"I have nothing to give," she said sadly, "nothing at all—no coins, no jewels."

The man turned away. But before he had limped more than a few steps, Brigid called him back.

"Here, take this sword. You can sell it for a great deal of money. Get food and medicine for yourself, and then share the rest with other people who are in need."

"I may be arrested for a thief if I try to sell such a thing as that," said the man fearfully.

"No," said Brigid. "It will be all right. Tell the dealer in the town that Brigid, the king's daughter, gave it to you."

Hardly had the beggar disappeared down the road than Brigid's father and Dunlaing came out of the house. The king strode ahead to get his sword—and of course it was not there!

"A poor, sick man came by while you were gone," explained Brigid. "I had no coins or jewels or anything at all to give him, so I gave him your sword."

Her father's face grew as hard as the sound of thunder. Dunlaing would certainly not want to marry Brigid after this!

"You can see why I want to get rid of her!" he raged. "I can't afford to keep her."

"Neither could I," said Dunlaing, looking amused, "for if she gives away her father's goods, she would certainly give away her husband's."

"Indeed I would!" said Brigid cheerfully. "I would give the whole kingdom to the poor, if I could."

Dunlaing stood looking at her. He was a wise and good young

man, and he could see that Brigid was someone special.

"I think this girl is important to God," he said slowly to her father. "I think it is not for you or me to decide what she is to do with her life. I am sure God has plans for her."

Brigid's father was still furious. He drove his daughter home without saying another word. Brigid was sorry that he was annoyed—but what else could she have done? And she was very glad that there was no more danger of her being made to marry Dunlaing. She too, was sure that God had plans for her, and that she would be allowed to carry them out in the end.

And she was right, of course. When her father got over his anger, he decided that there would be no peace for him until he let her have her way. So it was not many days later that he told her he would grant her wish. He would take her to the Bishop and let her consecrate her whole life to Christ.

Before Christianity had come to Ireland, the people had been pagans. The pagan priests, called druids, used to light sacred fires, which were kept burning for a certain length of time. Young girls were chosen to tend the fires and see that they did not go out. These girls lived together in a house set apart for their use. So now,

when Brigid said that she and other girls who were giving their whole lives to God wanted to live together in a house of their own, it did not seem a strange or new idea to the Irish people.

But first, Brigid and those who wanted to go with her walked in a procession to the church. Joy made Brigid so lovely that people gasped to see her. There is a legend that when she stood in front of the altar, she rested her hand on the wooden rail; and though the wood was dead and dry, it came alive and sent out leaves. It had received new life from the warmth of Brigid's love for God!

Brigid founded the first convent in Ireland. It was in a part of the country called Connaught. There she and the other nuns taught the Faith to young and old. Before long, soldiers, priests, Bishops, farmers—all sorts of people—were coming to ask her advice. She was not much more than twenty years old, but she was very wise in heavenly wisdom. And she had sensible advice to give about things of the world, too.

Many grateful people sent gifts to the convent—food, animals for the farm, and even bags of gold. Brigid gave the gold away at once, and most of the food. Her Sisters were sometimes hungry,

but never too hungry, sometimes cold, but never too cold. And they were always happy be-cause they belonged to God and because Brigid, their leader, was wise, and kind, and good.

Brigid's fame spread far and wide, and soon people from all parts of Ireland were begging her to come and start schools and convents for them. From Connaught she went to Leinster, where she built a church and convent near some oak trees. This place she called Kildare, which means Church of the Oak.

It was soon crowded with people, who came to pray with Brigid and to ask for her prayers. She opened a school, and that was crowded too. And, of course, the poor people she loved so much soon found her and came asking for charity.

Chieftains, Bishops, beggars—all came to Kildare to see Brigid. And they often had to go out into the fields to find her where she was tending the cows. The rest of the world might think of her as the great lady, Abbess of Kildare, but she still thought of herself as an ordinary working woman with a great deal of work to do for God.

One cold, blustery day she was in the fields with her herd of cows. Her big shawl was wrapped around her and the corner

pulled up over her head like a hood. A little boy called Ninnid ran through the field on his way to school.

"Little boy, why are you running?" Brigid called.

"I'm on my way to Heaven," he said pertly. He had no idea who the bundled-up cowherd was.

"Will you stop and pray with me that I may go, too?"

"I can't," said Ninnid. "The gates are open now but if I don't hurry they may be shut against me."

He really meant that he was afraid of being late for school. But for some reason Brigid didn't understand it that way.

"Come and pray with me," she insisted. "You pray that I

may find the gates of Heaven open, and I will pray that you may go through them when your time comes."

Although he did not know who she was, there was something about Brigid that made Ninnid do as she asked. So they knelt on the windswept hillside among the cows and said a prayer together. Then Ninnid ran on to school. He was in good time, after all, and he did very well in his lessons that day.

She was asked to start other schools and convents in many parts of the land. When she traveled about, it was always through a crowd. At home in Kildare it seemed as if all Ireland was coming to see her. A whole village of houses grew up there to provide shelter for the people who came.

One day a woman called on Brigid bringing a pretty little girl with her. Brigid took the child's hand and said, "What are you going to be when you grow up?"

The child didn't answer but her mother did.

"She was born dumb," the woman said. "She has never been able to speak."

"I'm going to hold her hand until she does," said Brigid with a smile. Then she asked the child again, "What are you going to be when you grow up?"

"Whatever you think I should be," replied the little girl in a clear voice.

The mother gasped.

"She spoke! They told me she never would, that she could not! Oh, thank God! Thank God !"

"Yes, we should thank Him indeed," Brigid agreed.

"Could I stay here and go to your school and be a Sister when I grow up?" the little girl asked.

"Of course you can stay here and go to school if your mother would like you to," said Brigid. "But as for being a Sister, well, we shall have to see what God decides about that."

Brigid spent many years in this busy life. She was as strong and steady as the Wicklow Hills she loved so much. People used to say she was very like them, for she pointed to heaven but kept her feet firmly on earth.

Her steps grew a little slower. When she took the cows to pasture now, she walked ahead of them saying her prayers or plaiting the rush crosses. And the cows followed obediently. As a rule, someone had to walk behind them to keep them from straying; but with Brigid, even when her back was turned on them, they never stepped off the path.

More and more people came to consult with her. Most of the callers had a good reason for coming, but a few came just so they could say they had talked with the great Lady Abbess of Kildare. They hoped to hear her say deep spiritual things. Then they could quote her words and impress their neighbors. But Brigid knew this sort of person as soon as she saw one.

Now she had a saying, and a wise one, that she repeated often. But to these vain visitors she would say it with a twinkle in her eye, well knowing that it was much too simple to please them. "Have sense," she would say, "take food, seek God, and there's no fear on you."

"There's no fear on you" is a nice Irish way of saying, "You have nothing to be afraid of."

And having said that, Brigid would go back to her prayers or off to her cows. The stupid people—vain people are always stupid—would feel cheated, never knowing they had been given a fine plan for a good life.

Many of the children who had first been taught in Brigid's schools were grown up now. Some had married and had children of their own, who were going to Brigid's schools in their turn. Others had entered one of her convents and were teaching there. Among the boys she had helped, many had become priests. Little Ninnid, who had prayed with her as she herded cows on the cold hillside long ago, was a missioner. He traveled to far countries, bringing the word of God to people who had never heard of Him before.

Ninnid had been surprised when he had learned that it was Brigid he had met that day. But he had never stopped praying, as she had asked, that when her time came she would find the gates of Heaven open for her.

In late January in the year 523, Ninnid was returning from his travels. As soon as he set foot on shore, a messenger ran up to

him with word that Brigid was very sick and wanted to see him.

"But how could she possibly know I was here?" asked Ninnid. "Why, I have barely arrived!"

"And she is getting ready to depart," said the messenger sadly. "She wants you to see to her going."

Ninnid didn't wait to hear any more. He borrowed a horse and set out at once to be with Brigid when she died.

A bitter cold had clamped down on the land but Ninnid didn't feel it. The horse's breath turned to steam and then froze in small icicles on his muzzle. Ninnid's hands seemed made of stone. But he pushed the horse faster and faster, praying, as they clattered along the ice-hard road and over frozen fields, that they would be in time.

Brigid was too weak to speak to him when he finally entered her room. But she smiled. And her eyes followed him as he brought the holy oils to anoint her. She managed to move a little on her narrow plank bed so that he could reach her more easily. The next day, February 1, she died.

There was great grief all through Ireland when people learned that their beloved Brigid had left them. The poor remembered how much she had done for them. The sad remembered the comfort she had given them. The wise were distressed that Brigid, so much wiser than any of them, would guide them no more. In the field, the cows wandered restlessly—as if they were looking for the gentle lady who used to pray and plait crosses as she tended them.

But among the people, along with the sadness there soon came a feeling of safety. They knew that the words she had said to the boy Ninnid long ago were meant for everyone. They were sure that everyone who prayed with Brigid would find the gates of Heaven open when it was time for them to leave this world.